I0763194

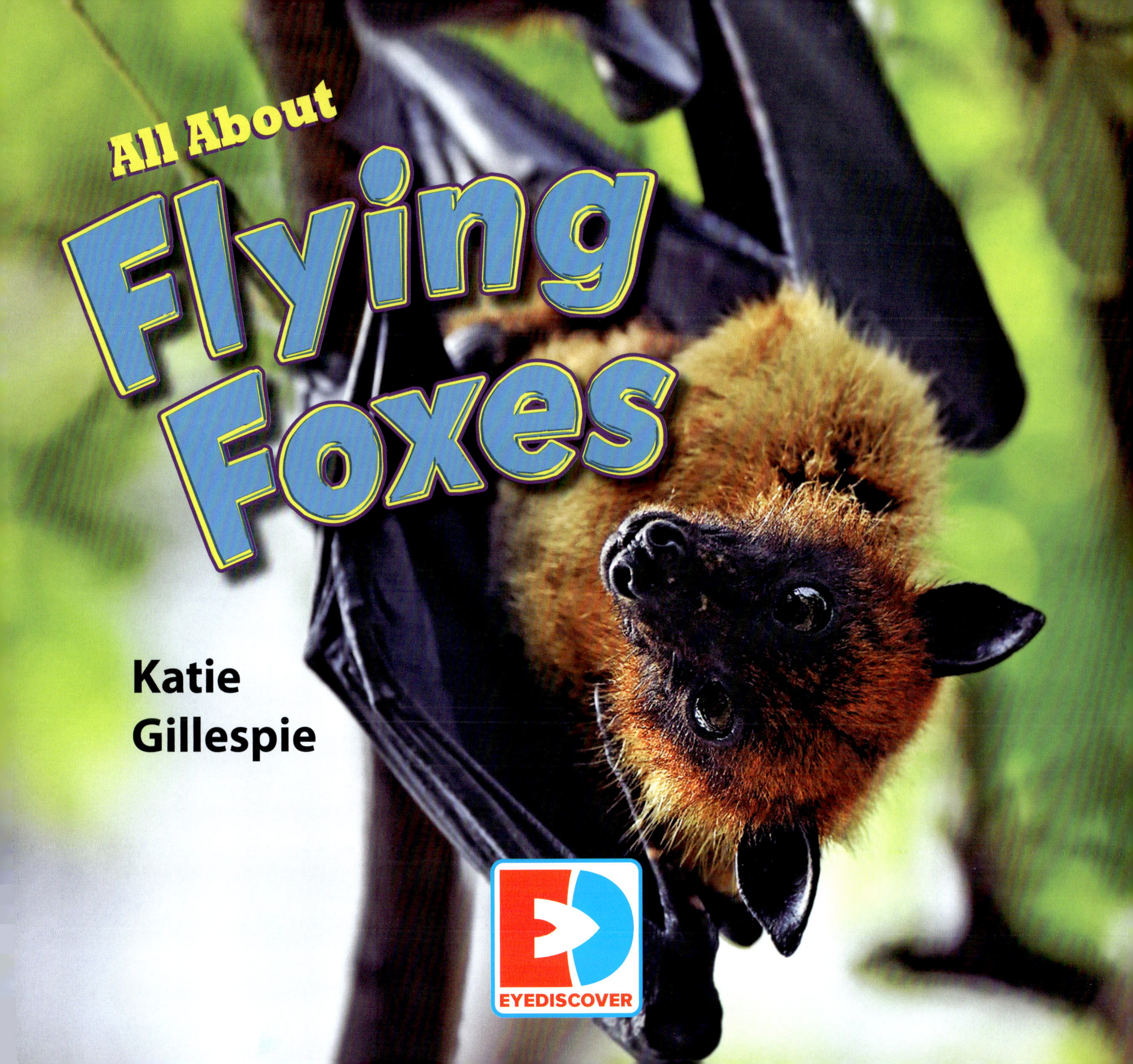
All About
Flying Foxes
Katie
Gillespie
EYEDISCOVER

Go to **www.eyediscover.com** and enter this book's unique code.

BOOK CODE

B264393

EYEDISCOVER brings you optic readalongs that support active learning.

EYEDISCOVER provides enriched content, optimized for tablet use, that supplements and complements this book. EYEDISCOVER books strive to create inspired learning and engage young minds in a total learning experience.

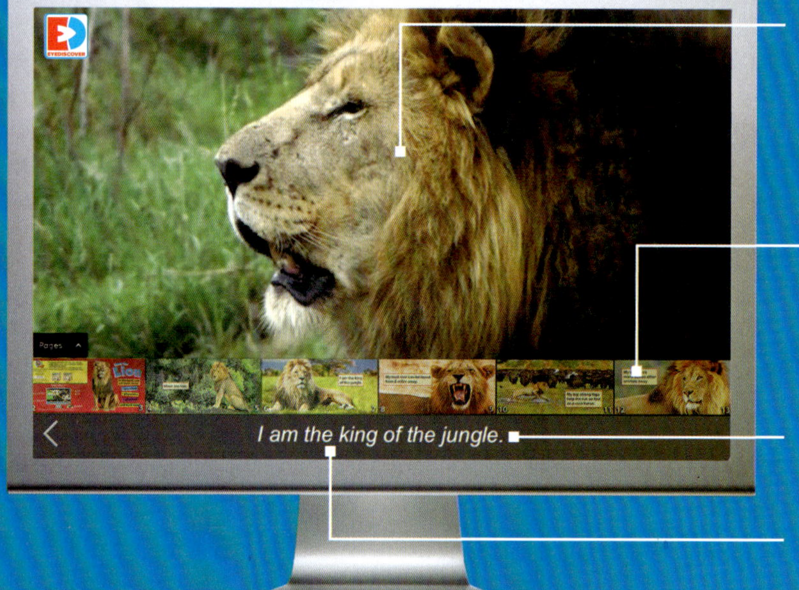

Watch
Video content brings each page to life.

Browse
Thumbnails make navigation simple.

Read
Follow along with text on the screen.

Listen
Hear each page read aloud.

Your EYEDISCOVER Optic Readalongs come alive with...

Audio
Listen to the entire book read aloud.

Video
High resolution videos turn each spread into an optic readalong.

OPTIMIZED FOR

- TABLETS
- WHITEBOARDS
- COMPUTERS
- AND MUCH MORE!

Published by AV² by Weigl
350 5th Avenue, 59th Floor New York, NY 10118
Website: www.eyediscover.com

Library of Congress Control Number: 2017930711

ISBN 978-1-4896-5653-7 (hardcover)

Printed in the United States of America
in Brainerd, Minnesota
1 2 3 4 5 6 7 8 9 0 21 20 19 18 17

022017
020317

Editor: Katie Gillespie
Designer: Mandy Christiansen

Weigl acknowledges Getty Images, iStock, Alamy, and Shutterstock as the primary image suppliers for this title.

All About

Flying Foxes

In this book, you will learn about

- how they look
- what they eat
- where they live

and much more!

Flying foxes are a kind of bat. Bats are the only mammals that can fly.

Flying foxes have fox-like faces. This is where their name comes from.

Flying foxes live in Australia and Asia. They make their homes in tropical rainforests.

Flying foxes are very big. They are the largest bats on Earth.

Bats hang upside down to rest or sleep. This is called roosting.

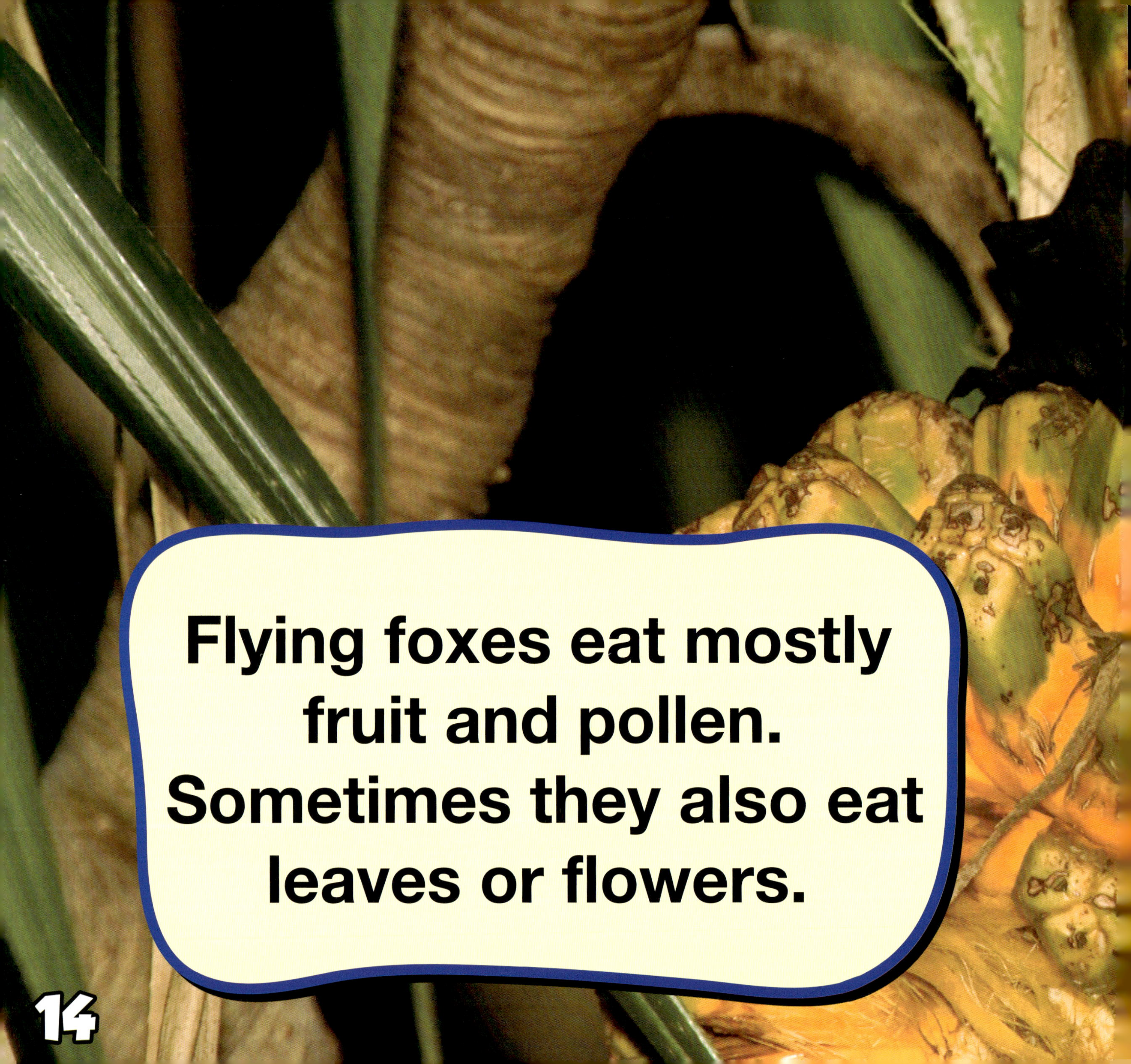

Flying foxes eat mostly fruit and pollen. Sometimes they also eat leaves or flowers.

Flying foxes carry seeds and pollen. This helps plants grow in new places.

Flying foxes can see and hear very well. These senses help them find their way.

Some trees can not grow without flying foxes. It is important for people to leave them alone.

Bats make up 25% of all mammals on Earth.

Flying foxes are the **heaviest bats in the world** at up to 3.3 pounds. (1.5 kilograms)

Female flying foxes give birth to one baby each year.

A flying fox's **wingspan** can be about **6 feet wide**.

This is as wide **as a person is tall**. (1.8 meters)

Four kinds of **flying foxes** live in **mainland Australia**.

Flying foxes start to fly when they are **8 to 10 weeks old**.

KEY WORDS

Research has shown that as much as 65 percent of all written material published in English is made up of 300 words. These 300 words cannot be taught using pictures or learned by sounding them out. They must be recognized by sight. This book contains 55 common sight words to help young readers improve their reading fluency and comprehension. This book also teaches young readers several important content words, such as proper nouns. These words are paired with pictures to aid in learning and improve understanding.

Page	Sight Words First Appearance
4	a, are, can, kind, of, only, that, the
7	comes, faces, from, have, is, name, their, this, where
8	and, homes, in, live, make, they
11	big, earth, on, very
13	down, or, to
14	also, eat, leaves, sometimes
16	carry, grow, helps, new, places, plants
19	find, hear, see, them, way, well
20	for, important, it, not, people, some, these, trees, without

Page	Content Words First Appearance
4	bat, flying foxes, mammals
8	Asia, Australia, rainforests
13	roosting
14	flowers, fruit, pollen
16	seeds
19	senses

Watch
Video content brings each page to life.

Browse
Thumbnails make navigation simple.

Read
Follow along with text on the screen.

Listen
Hear each page read aloud.

Go to www.eyediscover.com and enter this book's unique code.

BOOK CODE

B 2 6 4 3 9 3